W9-CAX-803

THE LOST CROWN OF SODOR

Illustrated by Tommy Stubbs

A Random House PICTUREBACK® Book

Random House 🏠 New York

Thomas the Tank Engine & Friends™

CREATED BY BRITT ALLCROFT

Based on The Railway Series by The Reverend W Awdry.

ISBN 978-0-449-81533-5

randomhouse.com/kids   www.thomasandfriends.com

Printed in the United States of America
10 9 8 7 6 5 4 3 2

HiT entertainment

It was a busy day at Brendam Docks. Thomas and Percy were shunting trucks. One of the trucks bashed into Percy's buffer and tipped over. A crate fell out and split open.

"Look!" peeped Percy. "It's a metal man, a robot!"

"Silly," Cranky grumbled. "It's a suit of armor, like a knight used to wear."

"Cranky's right," said Sir Topham Hatt. "In the old days, the Island of Sodor was ruled by kings. The most beloved was King Godred. He lived in Ulfstead Castle and wore a golden crown. The crown disappeared long ago."

Sir Topham Hatt said that the ruins of Ulfstead Castle
could be seen on the Earl of Sodor's estate.

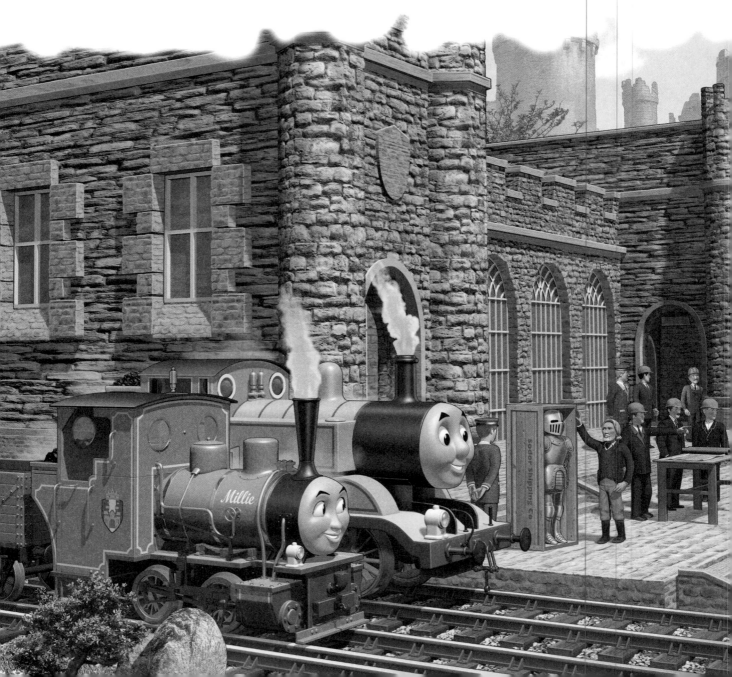

The next morning, Thomas delivered a crate to the earl's estate.
There he met Millie, the earl's Narrow Gauge engine.
"If only I had King Godred's golden crown," the earl said sadly.

Over the next few days, Thomas, James, and Percy made many deliveries to the earl's estate. Thomas saw his friend Jack the Digger there.

"I'm helping the earl restore Ulfstead Castle," Jack puffed.

"So *that's* his plan!" whistled Thomas.

When Thomas, Percy, and James were shunting containers, Thomas
saw a flatbed holding a very large crate. The earl said it was a special
delivery for the Steamworks. He climbed into Thomas' cab, and the three
friends pulled the crate to the Steamworks.

When they got there, a gantry crane lifted the crate to reveal an old engine named Stephen. His wood was worn, and he had rust holes in his boiler. He hadn't run in years.

"Surprise!" the old engine peeped.

Victor said he'd have Stephen fixed up in no time.

The earl told Thomas he had a special job for Stephen.

"But it's best not to say anything yet."

"I won't say a word," said Thomas. "I promise."

Victor worked quickly. Soon Stephen was good as new.

"You look Really Useful again," Thomas peeped.

Stephen had told the engines about his early days. "I worked so fast they called me the Rocket!" he said.

But what job would he do now?

As the others rolled away to work, Thomas saw that Stephen looked sad. So Thomas broke his promise and told Stephen that the earl had a special job for him.

Stephen was very excited.

Thomas, James, and Percy steamed to the earl's estate.

Inside the castle walls, they were amazed to see a giant platform on rails. The earl called it the traveler.

"You three will move the traveler into place for the men. You must be careful to keep the platform stable."

Meanwhile, Stephen wanted to know about his special job, so he rolled off to Brendam Docks.

"There's no work here for an old engine like you," Cranky said.

Next, Stephen went to Blue Mountain Quarry.

"We can always use help," Luke peeped.

But the trucks Stephen tried to pull were too heavy. He steamed and strained, but they wouldn't move.

"When I worked in a mine, the trucks weren't this heavy," said Stephen. "Are there any mines around here?"

Skarloey told him there was an old mine near the castle ruins. "I don't think anyone works there now," he said.

Stephen found the entrance to the abandoned mine. He sighed.

"There's no job on this island for me!"

Nearby, Thomas was working with the Troublesome Trucks. Suddenly, the trucks slipped loose and roared down the hill, right toward Stephen! Stephen had no choice but to push into the mine. His funnel hit the roof and fell off. Rocks crashed down behind him, sealing up the entrance.

Stephen searched for a way out. He crept around dark bends and through empty tunnels, but the tracks just went in circles. The only thing he found was an old wooden crate.

Thomas and Percy searched for Stephen. At the entrance
to the old mine, Thomas saw something familiar lying on
the ground. It was Stephen's funnel!

Thomas chuffed away to get Jack the Digger. Jack cleared the mine entrance, and Thomas raced in.

"Stephen! Stephen!" he peeped.

Stephen heard Thomas, but he was too weak to move or even whistle.

Finally, Thomas turned a corner and saw a welcome sight.

Thomas pushed Stephen out of the mine. The earl was there to greet them.

"I found a big wooden chest in the mine," Stephen said.

"Wonderful!" the earl exclaimed. "But first we must get you ready for tomorrow. You are an engine with a special job to do!"

The next day, an excited crowd gathered around
Ulfstead Castle.
"Welcome, ladies and gentlemen, engines and coaches,"
said the earl.

"Let me introduce my special steam engine, Stephen! He and Millie will be happy to show you the grounds."

Stephen's new funnel glittered like gold. It reminded Thomas of something.

"Stephen found something I thought was lost forever," the earl said. "King Godred's long-lost crown!"

Thomas realized what Stephen's funnel looked like—a crown! The engines cheered for Stephen. He wasn't the fastest or the strongest, but he was Really Useful—and today he was a king!